EARNING HER LOVE

SWEET SOMETHINGS BOOK TWO

RORY REYNOLDS

Earning Her Love

(Sweet Somethings Book 2)

Rory Reynolds © 2020

Cover by Popkitty Designs

❀ Created with Vellum

to everyone who struggles... you're seen

PROLOGUE
MARGO

WHERE THE HECK IS LANI? She was supposed to be here an hour ago to help me get ready. For the hundredth time, I'm questioning the wisdom of having an actual booth at the Apple Festival. Yeah, it'll be great for our small town of Sugarhill to bring in business from our neighboring town of Clearwater, but this is so not my thing. I'd rather be at my bakery serving up treats than here where there are dozens upon dozens of tourists who come to the festival every year.

I'm setting up the last of my mini apple pies when disaster strikes. The cheap table that the festival coordinator assigned me wobbles, and in the next second, two of the legs buckle. My first thought is 'oh, crap' my next is lord, this is going to be a disaster. I rush to grab the end of the table before all is lost, and I end up with a pile of apple desserts on the ground.

Of course, that means that instead of hitting the ground, they slide off the table and onto me. Soon enough, I'm covered in apple pie filling and sticky apple-honey from my apple-honey cinnamon rolls.

I do my best to hold up the end of the table while not letting anything else slide, but the table is freakin' heavy and awkward on the soft grass of the field the festival is held in. Despite the fact that I'm clearly struggling, not a single person comes to my rescue. No, the other people selling their sweets and baked goods either completely ignore my situation or snicker at my predicament.

Crap.

Tears swim in my eyes, and I consider just dropping the darn table and letting it fall so I can get out of here and back to Sprinkled With Sugar. The baker in me can't let so many of the desserts I slaved over for the last two days to be ruined. I nearly release my grip on the table when two big, strong arms encircle me from behind, and large hands grip the table on either side of my much smaller ones.

"I've got it, sweetness." My eyes fall closed at the comforting rumble of Amos' voice in my ear. "You can let go."

I nod and duck under his arm. "Thank you," I say with a shy smile.

I move quickly, pulling all of my desserts from the broken table and set them back on the cart I wheeled them over on. Once it's empty, Amos puts the table's broken end on the ground and wipes his hands on his jeans to try and get the sticky pie filling from his hands. It's then that I remember my own run-in with the desserts and look down at myself. I groan because I'm covered in apple pie filling and crumbs from the crusts. Not only on my clothes, but I somehow have apple-honey glaze in my hair.

"You okay?" Amos asks, obviously concerned. Probably because I'm once again staring at him like an idiot —something I do way too often in his presence. I can't help it. He's the sexiest man alive. If I could build the perfect man, he wouldn't be half as gorgeous as Amos Webster.

No, my imagination isn't good enough to come up with those fathomless hazel eyes and the sharp cut of his scruffy jaw. I've never considered myself the kind of woman who would swoon over such a big, gruff man, but here we are. I can't get the image of his muscular chest and that sexy V that trails down to the promised lands out of my mind.

I've only seen him shirtless one time, and it's burned into my memory. He was out jogging with only a pair of loose shorts that hung low on his hips. A hot and sweaty Amos is nothing to turn your nose at. Nope, all I could imagine is what it would be like to be underneath someone so big and powerful with his corded muscles and overall bulk.

My imagination runs wild anytime I think about that day. I can't even tell you how many times my hands have snuck into my panties to the image of him stalking towards me in those gray running shorts with fire in his hazel eyes—those green and gold flecks burning bright just for me. My friends think I have a crush on Amos, but it's so much more than that. I lust after the man in a major way. Not to mention despite his gruff, almost rude behavior towards just about everyone, I'm half in love with him. Him coming to my rescue today is just another moment in a long line of little things he's done over the last year that have made my heart flip.

"I'm fine... a little sticky, but not hurt. Well, maybe my pride."

Amos chuckles. "Sticky is a good look on you."

My core clenches at the double meaning. That's another thing about Amos... he is a terrible flirt but in this covert kind of way. Everything is an innuendo. He never straight up says anything that could be considered inappropriate, but there's always this underlying sexual implication to his words that has my panties self-combusting every time he's near.

"Thanks... I think?"

He licks his lips. "Oh, it's definitely a compliment, sweetness."

My cheeks flush with embarrassment. I might have a million dirty thoughts about Amos Webster, but I'm definitely not the type of girl to flirt ostentatiously like he does. I'm not sure what changed... maybe seeing our friends Lani and Torin finally figure out their own relationship has pushed him toward more openly showing his intentions, but I'm not complaining.

It turns out my friends were right. They've been telling me for months that Amos is as attracted to me as I am him, but I never saw it. Yes, he bought desserts from my bakery even though his diner is famous for their own desserts. Yes, he personally picked them up every morning when he could have easily sent one of his employees, but the man was a real jerk about it.

Every morning he opened the boxes of treats and counted them and looked them over like some quality control Nazi. Then he would grunt and leave with his box of desserts.

Frankly, it pissed me off and made me feel like an idiot for wanting him so dang bad. Now, I think he was so gruff and standoffish because he's as affected by me as I am him. The tension has been building for months now, and it's only a matter of time before it explodes.

"Well, thank you then. And thanks for saving my hard work. None of these other jerks made a move to help me, just gawked like it'd be one more competitor down. I knew this was a bad idea."

Amos shakes his head. "It's a great idea. It's not your fault that they gave you a shitty table. It's definitely not your fault that these assholes," he turns and levels a nasty glare at several of the surrounding business owners, "would lift a selfish finger to help a woman in distress, regardless of how beautiful she is."

My cheeks flush pink at the compliment. That's another thing that's changed. He's continuously complimenting me. Not my baked goods—me. It's a heady thing having a man like Amos compliment me. I've never had low self-esteem, but I'm a realist. I'm not nearly as thin as the ideal woman. My hair is a curly black tornado. No matter how much I try to straighten it, the curl bounces right back, and then it frizzes as if I offended it in attempting to tame my curls. I'm pretty, I guess, but definitely not in his league. He deserves some kind of supermodel hanging off his arm, not a curvy small-town baker who eats way too many of her own creations.

"I really appreciate it," I say, trying to unsuccessfully clean myself up with the paper-thin napkins I brought for customers. The only thing I've managed to do is spread the stickiness and get bits of napkin stuck in the mess.

Amos closes the few feet that separate us, my heart pounds in my chest at his nearness. That's one line he hasn't crossed. He's never gotten into my space. Flirted, yes. Touched no. He lifts his hand toward my face, and my breath arrests in my chest as the anticipation grows. Oh, God, he's going to touch me.

His thumb glides across my cheek and comes away with a bit of pie filling. I could die of embarrassment... that is, until he lifts his thumb to his mouth and sucks it off his finger.

Holy crap, that's hot. My core heats, and my panties grow wet at the sight. He lets out a little growl of approval as if that little taste of pie filling is the best thing he's ever tasted. He stares down at me with heated eyes, his lips slowly lowering to mine. My eyes fall closed, and I tip my head back ever so slightly, telling him I'm on board for his kiss.

"Sorry, I'm late!" Lani calls out as she comes rushing up.

Amos takes a frustrated step away from me. I instantly miss the heat that radiated off of him. I definitely miss the almost-kiss. With a sigh, I greet my best friend. She's positively glowing. I've heard that pregnancy can do that to a girl, but I think it's more about the man walking a couple steps behind his whirlwind of a wife. Yeah, Torin and Lani are the perfect couple who radiate love and happiness.

"What happened?" Lani asks with wide eyes.

I shake my head. "It's a long story…"

1

MARGO

My alarm goes off, and I slap it with a groan. Three A.M. comes early. Especially the day after book club... which at this point has devolved into drinking wine and eating the leftover desserts from my bakery. We might as well call it sugar-coma night instead, but Lani insists on keeping up pretenses. I slowly drag myself from my bed and make my way to the shower. I strip off my sleep shirt and flick on the cold water before stepping inside. The burst of freezing cold does its job and jolts my system awake. I adjust the temperature and relax into the steady stream of hot water. Minutes later, I'm dressed and have my hair twisted up into a tight bun.

Fifteen minutes later, I'm letting myself into the back door of the bakery and flicking on the coffee machine. I do my normal prep for the day while my coffee percolates. I've got the ovens preheating and the ingredients ready for my first recipe of the morning. I take my first sip of liquid goodness with a little sigh.

Before I know it, two hours have passed, and it's time to put together the first special orders of the day. I leave packaging Burnt Sugar's order until last. As always, I make sure every dessert in the box is perfect. Every double chocolate chip cookie is perfectly round. The mini pies are golden brown perfection. Even the cinnamon rolls are completely even in size and have the exact amount of sticky apple-honey glaze.

Thirty minutes after I open the doors, all the special orders have been picked up but for one. Amos always waits to pick up Burnt Sugar's order until after the morning rush trickles out. Like clockwork, the bell above the door dings and in strides the object of my infatuation. He's wearing a Burnt Sugar Diner t-shirt which is stretched taut over his muscular chest and a pair of jeans that hang low on his hips. I can't help but wonder how much of his tanned, tattooed skin would show if he lifted his arms.

I lick my lips at the fantasy, cursing the fact that I don't need a lightbulb changed. He'd do it too, then I could spend the time gawking at his hotness without the risk of getting caught.

"Morning, sweetness."

"Good morning, Amos. I've got your order ready." I run to the back to grab the order and then promptly trip on my own feet a scant foot before I reach him with the cumbersome box. Like magic, Amos not only catches the box but manages to prevent me from taking a header too. He quickly sets the box on the counter then wraps both arms around me.

"Careful," he says in that sexy growl of his that does naughty things to my body. It never fails to turn me on.

"Thank you," I say, completely breathless and a little more than turned on like panty-melting levels of turned on. Ever since our interrupted moment at the Apple Festival a month ago, every moment I spend with him is fraught with sexual tension. I'm wound so tight it's a miracle that I haven't blown into a million pieces.

"You're welcome, sweetness."

Those hazel eyes of his are burning for me, maybe even with more need than last time he looked at me as if to warn me of his impending kiss. I don't need a warning though. I just need the dang kiss. I need it like I need my next breath. I'm so hungry for it that I'm tempted to close the distance myself, but I can't do that for some reason. I want Amos to make the first move.

His arms tighten around me, and my hands grip his shirt in tight fists. Slowly his mouth descends, and I know this is it. This, right here, is the moment that I kiss Amos Webster for the first time. And then like a cruel twist of fate, the bell above the door rings, announcing a customer.

I move away from Amos like I've been scalded— and I practically was from the heat between us. I have a feeling that a kiss from him will leave scars all over my heart. One of my best friends, Prue, stands just a foot inside the door gaping at us. She raises an eyebrow in question, and I give a minute shake of my head, telling her to leave it.

"Hey Margo, just stopping in to get a coffee and

muffin. I had an early emergency call, and I'm dying for some caffeine and sugar."

I expected Amos to grab his order and leave, but instead, he stands there like a silent sentry daring anyone to ask him to leave. Not that Prue would, she wants us to get together as much as any of my friends, even if she is anti-relationship. Which is why after I give her the muffin and coffee, she hightails it out of here with barely a goodbye instead of hanging around and chatting like usual.

As soon as the door closes behind her, Amos strides toward me with purpose. Before I can protest—not that I would—he's got me by the hand and is dragging me to the kitchen. The doors swing shut behind us, and he smashes his lips to mine in a searing kiss.

2

AMOS

Iᴛ's my favorite part of the day—time to pick up my order from Sprinkled With Sugar. Time to see Margo. The woman that I'm completely gone for and desperate to have a taste of.

"Going to pick up my order from Margo's," I shout back through the pass-thru to Daisy.

"You finally gonna make your move on that pretty little baker?" she hollers back.

I ignore her little dig. She's been at me for over a year to make my move. It's not that I haven't wanted to; it's that the timing never seems right. Plus, until recently, Margo has been standoffish. Now I'm seeing that it isn't because she doesn't want me, it's because she wants me and is worried that I don't want her. It's time to erase that doubt because I definitely want her, and not just to slake my lust. I want so much more.

It's a quick walk across the street to the bakery. Thankfully, the rush is over—totally planned on my part—and if it goes my way, we will have several uninterrupted minutes together. Today's the day I taste her sweet lips.

The bells ding as I enter, and Margo shouts from the kitchen that she'll be right out. She pushes through the doors and comes to a dramatic halt as she realizes it's me. I don't think it's a surprise though. I always come as soon as the rush is over. When she looks me up and down licking her lips, I know it's not because she's surprised.

As she takes her time looking me over, I shamelessly do the same. My little baker is curvy in all the right places. Her hips are perfect for gripping as I fuck her. That ass of hers is a wet dream. Her tits are full and round, begging to be worshiped. I would worship at their altar for hours if I had half a chance. I end my perusal on her cupid's bow mouth. Her lips are pillowy, and I can't help imagining what they would look like spread around my cock.

Fuck.

My cock is achingly hard behind my zipper. Margo's eyes land on my bulge and become hooded. I guarantee she's wet for me. I lick my lips, imagining her taste on my tongue. She'd be sweeter than those treats she sells me every day.

"Morning, sweetness," I say, breaking the spell cast around us.

"Good morning, Amos. I've got your order ready." She practically jumps to attention as she turns and runs back into the kitchen to collect my order. Hop away, little rabbit... I'll catch you soon enough.

I see disaster coming before it strikes as Margo

rushes out of the swinging doors. I rush to her and catch the box of desserts seconds before it comes crashing to the floor. I set it on the counter and catch her up in my arms before she can hit the floor herself. Her breath rushes out as I pull her against my chest, wrapping both arms around her.

"Careful," I murmur lowly.

"Thank you..." she says breathlessly.

"You're welcome, sweetness."

Just as I'm about to crush my mouth to hers, the bell on the door dings, and Margo jumps away from me like she's been burned. Fuck me. It's her friend Prue. I swear those friends of hers are the biggest cockblockers in the world. First Lani and now Prue. Thankfully, Prue seems to catch the tension and gets her coffee and muffin and leaves quickly.

I don't hesitate a moment longer. I grab Margo's hand and drag her willing body to the kitchen. Before the door swings shut, I have her in my arms, and I'm kissing her like the starving man I am. I've craved her lips for longer than I'd like to admit, and my imagination didn't do her flavor justice. She tastes better than her sweetest dessert.

Her lips are just as soft as they appear and twice as delicious. I wrap my fingers around the back of her neck and tilt her head back so I can deepen the kiss. She willingly opens for me, and I get the first taste of her smooth tongue. Her tongue slicks against mine excitedly, and before I know what I'm doing, I have her lifted in my arms, and I'm striding across the kitchen and setting her sexy ass on the countertop.

"Amos... we can't..." I take her lips in another searing hot kiss, not letting her finish her protest. She rips her mouth away from me, panting. "Not here..." she tries to protest again, but I steal her words again with a kiss.

All pretense of argument flees from her body as she melts into me. Her legs wrap around me, and her hot little pussy grinds against my cock. We both groan at the contact, and our mouths become frantic. I'm so hard I could come in my jeans just from her rubbing against me like she is.

Like a glass of ice water dumped all over us, the bell over the door dings, and a customer calls out for help. I pull away, resting my forehead to hers as we try to catch our breaths. "It's like the world is conspiring against us."

She nods with a pout. "I think it is..."

"Helloooo," the customer yells out.

"Just a fucking minute," I growl.

Margo slaps her hand on my chest and gives me a dirty look that I kiss right off her face. She pulls away with a grumble then slides down my body as she hops down from the counter. She's halfway to the door when I twirl her around and lay another searing kiss on her pouty mouth.

"Have dinner with me."

Her eyes flash with indecision and something that looks a lot like longing. "I don't know..."

"Please, Margo."

She gives me a shy smile. "I don't think I've ever heard you say my name..."

I encircle her in my arms again. "Please, have dinner with me, Margo," I rasp in her ear. From the way she shivers, I can tell how much she's affected by me.

She nods. "Okay... when?"

"Excuse me, is anyone working in this place?!" the impatient customer calls.

"Be there in a second!" Margo says, sounding more annoyed than apologetic.

"Tonight, my place."

Her eyes heat at the implication. "Sounds good," she says lowly. "Tonight..."

I nod. "Tonight, sweetness."

———————

"MA, I don't need help getting a date."

"If you didn't need help, you'd be married and giving me grandbabies already. I'm not going to be around forever."

I do my best to hold in the long-suffering sigh that's trying to escape. "I have a date tonight," I confess. It's not like she won't hear it from Daisy, my mom's busybody best friend who still works at the diner even though she should've retired years ago.

"You do?" my mom says a little warily. "Who?"

"Margo Schultz, she owns Sprinkled With Sugar."

"Hmm... that the girl Daisy was going on about?"

I shake my head. "Ma, how am I supposed to know what that menace has or hasn't told you. I swear you move to Arizona, and you're more in my business than you were while you lived right here."

She laughs. "I just have to keep tabs on my baby boy."

"I'm thirty, I don't think I need tabs kept on me anymore."

"Ha! That's what you think. So when's the wedding?"

"Jesus, ma. We haven't even had a first date yet. Maybe tomorrow?" My words drip sarcasm, but something in my heart burns at the thought. Making Margo mine permanently, getting my ring on her finger—yeah, I like the sound of that.

"You need to settle down. Your dad won't be with us much longer, and you know how much he wants you to be happy."

My dad has Alzheimer's and is rapidly declining. It's one of the reasons they moved to Arizona. My dad wanted to stay here, but my mom insisted they move to be where the leading doctor that specializes in Alzheimer's lives. That's when I took over the diner. I didn't always see myself as a diner owner... I had other aspirations of my own, but family comes first, always.

It may not be a five Michelin star restaurant in New York, but Burnt Sugar Diner is exactly where I'm meant to be, even if I hadn't realized it. I love this town and the people in it. Aside from that, I never would've met Margo if I had run off to New York to become the next Ramsey. Margo is reason enough to never leave Sugarhill.

"I don't have to settle down to be happy."

My mom makes a tsking sound but doesn't respond. She knows I'm right; however we both want to do everything we can to make dad happy while he can remember us. Which is why they are coming for a visit in a couple weeks. Dad wants to spend some time in his hometown before he loses his lucidity completely.

"He just wants you to be as happy as we've been all these years." She sounds pained as she talks. I can't imagine watching the person you love most in the world fade away. Losing him one minute at a time.

"I know. Look, ma, I've got to go. Margo will be here soon, and I need to get dinner started."

"Love you, son. Talk soon."

"Love you too, ma. Hug dad for me."

At exactly seven o'clock, I hear the sound of a car door slamming. Margo is here. I half expected her to cancel on me, but here she is. When there isn't a knock on the door right away, I get curious and look out the window. Margo is standing on my porch... no, not standing, she's pacing in front of my door.

She walks to the door, raises her hand to knock, and then lets it fall again before pacing away. Her lips move as if she's talking to herself, and I can't help wondering what she's saying and if she's talking herself into or out of knocking. Not wanting to give her the easy out, I open the door. Margo jumps at the sound of the door opening and twirls around with wide eyes.

"Oh, hi."

I smirk at her and her awkwardness. My girl is a tigress hidden behind a shy kitten. I'm determined to draw that tigress from this morning out of her hiding place. I want to see her nails and feel her fierceness.

"Hello, sweetness. It looked like maybe you might be considering running away. Thought I would let you know that I'm willing to chase you if I have to."

Margo licks her lips, drawing my attention and making my cock twitch at the remembered taste of her. She tentatively takes a step towards me, then another, and another until she's directly in front of me. She looks up with wide green eyes. "I'm not running."

I give her a noncommittal shrug because it sure looked that way to me, but I'll let her think I believe her. "Good, because I've got dinner made, and I'd hate for you to miss out on the best stir fry you'll ever have."

3

MARGO

"THAT WAS the most amazing stir fry I've ever had." And it is. I've never tasted something with so many flavor notes that don't involve sugar, sugar, and more sugar.

"Glad you liked it, sweetness." If I didn't know better, I would say he's blushing, but a man like Amos wouldn't blush. "I've got burnt sugar pie for dessert."

My mouth waters. Burnt sugar pie is the only dessert that tops any of my confections. He sets a big slice of pie in front of me, and I don't wait a moment before taking a bite. "Mmm... this is so freakin' good."

He watches my mouth as I take another bite, my tongue swiping out to catch a stray crumb. My body heats at the look in his hazel eyes. He looks like he's ready for dessert, but not burnt sugar pie.

"You know, I've tried dozens of times to figure out the secret to this pie and haven't been able to even come close to replicating it."

Amos' lips quirk up. "It wouldn't be a secret recipe if it was easy to figure out."

"I suppose not," I say, then slowly lick the tines of my fork clean of the last bit of pie. "Can't blame a baker for trying."

He licks his lips, those dark, brooding eyes of his boring into mine as I lick my lips feeling wanton. I want him to want me as much as I do him. I don't want this night to end without us fully exploring the chemistry that burns bright in my belly.

I stand to carry our dishes to the sink, but he grips my wrist firmly, stopping me. "Those can wait," he growls.

My breath catches in my throat at the possessive grip. "For what?" I breathe out, quiet and needy.

"This," he says, dragging me into his lap and kissing me as if our lives depend on it. At this point, maybe they do. It feels so right being in his arms; kissing him feels natural and necessary.

Our tongues dance together, slick stroke after slick stroke. Over and over, our tongues caress... explore... My arousal grows until I know my panties are soaked through. My pussy throbs with how badly I need release. I turn in his lap so I'm straddling him. He groans as my pussy rubs against his hard cock. He feels enormous behind his zipper, something I didn't get to fully appreciate before we were interrupted this morning.

I break away from his lips, my head dropping back with a low moan as I roll my hips, mimicking what I want to do to him only without clothes. His big hands palm my ass and pull me tight against him, taking control of my movements. Just that one commanding touch has me spiraling towards an orgasm.

I love how he takes charge.

I know he'll be a beast in the bedroom, and I cannot wait to experience his fully unrestrained passion. He trails his mouth up and down my neck, first kissing then gently nipping at the sensitive skin. I shiver, loving his mouth on me but wanting more. So much more.

"Amos, I want you. Take me to bed."

He stops what he's doing, and I instantly regret talking. "Are you sure, sweetness? Once I have you laid out on my bed, I won't be able to stop myself. You'll be at my mercy."

"Yes, please. I'm yours."

Without another word, he lifts me up and over his shoulder as he storms towards what I assume is his bedroom. My breath whooshes out of my lungs when he tosses me on the bed. I squeal when he yanks me by the ankles to the edge of the bed. He makes quick work of removing my shoes and jeans.

"You're so fucking wet," he groans as he stares down at the wet spot on the gusset of my panties. From the way he's looking at the thing scrap of red lace I'm wearing, I'm extremely glad I took the time to go to Sugarhill's only boutique for some new lingerie.

I lick my lips. "You do that to me. You always have," I confess.

He growls, ripping the panties from my body. Not just pulling them off, he literally rips them from my body. So hot. I've never had a man want me so much that he can't control himself. I'm starting to think that Amos is everything I've ever wanted, not just out of bed, but in it too.

My back arches at the first swipe his tongue across my clit. I thread my fingers through his hair, telling him how much I love his mouth on me. He's eating me like he's starving and I'm the most delicious thing he's ever tasted. It's a heady feeling knowing how much he's enjoying eating my pussy. Most men go at it like a chore. Not Amos, he's licking and sucking at my pussy like he'll die without it.

"I'm going to come... Oh, God, your mouth feels so good." He growls into my pussy, redoubling his efforts as he drives me closer to my release. I'm right on the edge when he pushes two thick fingers inside me and immediately finds my g-spot. I scream as my orgasm ricochets through me, unable to control the sounds I'm making. I've never been a screamer, but apparently, I've never had a lover like Amos.

My orgasm subsides, and he pulls away, licking his fingers clean of my release. "Mmm delicious," he says, crawling up my body. He kisses me deeply, sharing my flavor with me. So dirty. I love it.

I push on his shoulder, and he willingly rolls over so that our positions are flipped, and I'm perched on top of his big body. I nip his chin as I make my way down his chest. I push his shirt up so I can see all those tattooed muscles. He pulls the shirt off, and I gasp at how perfect he looks.

My hands roam up and down his thick muscles, raking my fingertips over his nipples. He shudders, looking at me with hooded eyes. I follow the trail my hands are making with my mouth down his body to the top of his jeans. I undo his belt then his jeans. He lifts his hips helping me pull them down and off. His cock springs free. He's long and thick, beads of precome drip from his tip, trailing down his length.

My mouth waters. I've never wanted to suck a cock as much as I want his in my mouth. I take him in my hand, stroking him a few times before licking the drops from him. I look up at him as I slowly lave his cock. His head is thrown back, hands fisted in the bedding. I open my mouth and take the first couple inches, licking around the head as I lightly suck. His eyes pop open, and he looks down at me like a burning man.

I stroke him with my hand as I take him in my mouth, licking and sucking him deeper and deeper on every pass. I groan when his hands fist my hair, and his hips punch up, forcing more of his cock into my mouth. I greedily accept the extra inches, redoubling my efforts to take more of him.

"Fuck, your mouth is like heaven. Jesus. That's it, sweets, fucking suck my cock so good."

I hum around him loosening my jaw further so he can take full control. I have become nothing more than an outlet for his driving need. I love it. His restraint has snapped, and he's taking exactly what he wants, and I'm exhilarated. My hand slips down between my legs, and I tease my clit as I take him.

Using his firm grip on my hair, he pulls me up off of him, and I whimper. I want more. I don't want this to be over yet. I want to taste his release. I want to taste his loss of control as he comes down my throat. I pull against his hold, barely able to lick the tip of my tongue on the angry red head of his cock. He wants it as bad as I do, but he's got something else in mind, which becomes apparent when he lifts me bodily until I'm straddling his lap, his big cock a delicious tease between my legs.

I move up and down, spreading my wetness all over him. Fuck he's huge. I have a sliver of doubt that I can even take him. He's so much bigger than anyone I've ever been with, and it's as intimidating as it is arousing.

Amos strips me of my shirt and bra. I'm perched on his lap, rubbing my pussy wantonly on his cock, completely naked to him. From the look in his eyes, he loves what he's seeing. It does something to me that feels a lot less like lust and a whole lot more like another L-word. One that I am not even remotely ready to explore.

We've been tiptoeing around this thing for months now, but even so, it's too soon to think about anything more than a little bit of fun—okay, a whole lot of fun. I'm lost in sensation and don't realize his intentions until he's rolled us and is entirely in control again.

He kneels between my spread legs, rubbing the head of his cock around my clit then down to my entrance. I suck in a breath as his thick length slowly penetrates me. The feeling is one of pure, white-hot pleasure. He's stretching me so perfectly; all I can do is beg for more.

"Don't worry, sweetness, you're getting more," he says before pushing himself deep. I gasp at the intrusion. He's big. Huge, even. He stills, giving me time to adjust while his thumb rubs distracting circles around my clit. My muscles relax as he starts to slowly move.

"Heaven. Pure fucking heaven. Jesus, you're tight," he growls as my pussy grips him. "I'll never get enough of you." He punctuates each word with a thrust, each one getting more demanding and more relentless until he's fucking me in truth.

The orgasm comes from nowhere, barreling down on me like a freight train and splitting me apart at the edges. I scream his name, telling him to fuck me harder, not to stop. He pulls out and flips me to my hands and knees before plunging back inside, deeper than ever.

"Fuuuuck..." I cry out as he bottoms out, sending me into another orgasm. The orgasm goes on and on. I'm not sure if it's multiple orgasms or just one, unrelenting release. Stars dance behind my eyes, and my throat grows hoarse from calling out his name and telling him harder... don't stop... more.

My arms finally give out, and I crash to the mattress, my ass in the air while he fucks me to oblivion. I'm barely coherent when he pulls from me and groans as he comes across my ass and back. I can feel the hot release trailing down my thighs. It's deliciously dirty and a stark reminder that there was no condom. We didn't even talk about it. I've never been so irresponsible in my life, but I can't find it in myself to regret it. I'm on birth control, and I know deep in my heart that Amos wouldn't do anything to hurt me.

He kisses me between my shoulder blades before getting up from the bed. I'm basking in the bliss of multiple orgasms when Amos lifts me in his arms and carries me to the bathroom where he proceeds to gently and lovingly washes me in the shower. He dries me off then carries me back to bed. My whole body is languid and pliant. He crawls in behind me and pulls me tight against his chest. With a hum of pleasure at the feel of his big body wrapped around mine, I drift off to sleep.

I didn't intend to have a sleepover, but I'm definitely not moving now. Not when Amos has me cocooned in his arms.

4

AMOS

I WAKE up to Margo laying half on my chest, her leg thrown up over mine as she clings to me in her sleep. I can't figure out what woke me up until the sound persists. It's Margo's phone in the other room where she left her purse last night. I find the clock on my night-stand and see that it's three in the morning. It's then that I realize it's her alarm. I feel a little guilty for waking her twice in the night, trying to sate my insatiable appetite for her.

She groans and stretches as she wakes up. "Sorry to wake you up at this godawful hour," she says with an apologetic shrug. "Baker life."

I kiss the top of her head. "It's okay, sweets. Let's get cleaned up and off to work."

She gives me a confused look but doesn't say anything. What she doesn't realize is that today I'm coming with her. I'm off at the diner, and I want to spend the day with my girl. Plus, my little baker wants to learn how to make my family's secret recipe. It's a perfect excuse to get to spend the day with her.

I lick my lips, admiring my girl in a pair of my running shorts and t-shirts. The shorts had to be cinched up tight, but there's nothing that can make the shirt fit. It hangs off of her shoulder, showing an enticing amount of skin. Skin that I want to put my mouth on—skin that's already slightly pink from my beard rubbing against her. My cock thickens at the reminder of how she got that beard burn... and all the other places my girl is wearing my marks.

"Quit looking at me like that, or I'll never get to the bakery," Margo scolds. The hooded look she gives me, and the spark in her green eyes tells me that she wants more too.

"Sugarhill can live without muffins for one day..."

She shakes her head. "You're a menace. I'm already running late."

I shrug entirely unrepentant. Never has a shower been so wonderful as one with Margo's naked, soapy body rubbing all over mine. No man on Earth could resist such temptation—not that she put up any protest either.

"Let's get going then, sweetness. Wouldn't want to deny the townsfolk their muffins."

She snorts a laugh but slips her shoes on and grabs her purse. "Glad it's too dang early for anyone to see my walk of shame," she says, waving her hand up and down her body.

I pull her into my arms and kiss her deeply. "Nothing shameful about leaving my bed."

The dreamy look on her face says that she agrees. "You're right. I've just never done the whole one-night stand thing..."

I growl, taking a handful of her wild black hair and fisting it. "This is not a one-night stand. This is just the start of a lot of nights."

This is the start of forever, I think to myself.

Margo's eyes widen. "Oh... I just thought..."

"Whatever you're thinking, get it out of your mind right now. We're not nearly over yet."

Something in that bright-eyed smile she was wearing dims for some reason making her smile look a bit forced. "I need to get to the bakery."

I give her one more quick kiss before leading her out to her car. I open the driver's side door, helping her in before striding to the passenger side. I slide in without a word. It looks like she wants to ask why I'm in her car instead of taking my truck, but she just shrugs and starts the car.

It only takes a few minutes before she's parking behind Sprinkled With Sugar. One of the many perks of small-town life. You can get anywhere you want to go in ten minutes or less. I guide her to the backdoor, not liking how dark it is back here. Yes, our town is relatively safe, but all the dark shadows behind the building scream danger. I make a note to fix that. My girl's safety is my top priority.

Margo was shocked that I didn't just kiss her and head to the diner. I explained that it was only fair that I stay and help since it's my fault she's starting the day late. She gives me a wolfish grin. She's not one bit remorseful for the fact that she's running behind. Especially not for such a worthy reason. And me touching, tasting, and taking her body is definitely a worthy cause. My half-hard cock certainly agrees.

The first thing Margo does is change out of my clothes into a spare set of jeans and Sprinkled With Sugar t-shirt she keeps in her office. I'm disappointed to see her out of my clothes. I love having her in my clothes, something I hope to see often.

I stand to one side of the kitchen, watching dough spin in an industrial sized mixer. She explained that she rarely uses it, preferring small batches, but today she has an order for three hundred cookies, making her small-batch preference impossible.

My attention is once again caught by Margo and how she moves around her kitchen. She's like a choreographed dancer, moving from one task to another in a fluid, almost thoughtless motion. I can now understand why she put me in charge of this mixer, which needs zero supervision. I'm a distraction, and a hindrance to her perfectly choreographed dance. Despite my being in the way, she seems happy to have me here.

"It's weird having someone else here," she says out of the blue. "But I like it," she quickly adds.

"I've always wondered why you don't have Leanne in early to help you, but now I see," I wave my hands around the kitchen, "this is your kingdom and no one else belongs in the queen's chambers."

She laughs. "I'm no queen, and a hot bakery kitchen is certainly not a royal kingdom."

I cross the room to her and catch her up in my

arms. "You're most certainly a queen, and I am but your lowly servant."

Her eyes go all soft with desire. Her pink tongue dashes out and licks her bottom lip. "You're no servant... if anything, you're the king."

I growl, crushing my lips to hers. Our kiss quickly turns into an inferno between us. Her body lights up beneath my hands. My cock aches behind my zipper as she rubs against it. I break away, and we're both breathless. "I'll be your king, sweetness. You only have to ask."

Her pillowy bottom lip disappears between her lips, trying to hide the smile that I love so much. The one that until recently, she kept hidden under shyness whenever I was around. She's the one who kisses me this time, and once again, we fall into each other. This time when she pulls away, she's flushed and heavily lidded—aroused.

One of her many timers buzzes, breaking apart the sexual fog we were both becoming lost to. She jumps to attention and skitters off and continues her flawless dance around the kitchen. Leaving me to scoop perfectly round balls of chocolate chip cookies onto a dozen pans.

"You really don't have to stay and help. I'm sure you have things you need to get done at the diner."

"I know I don't have to stay. I want to. Besides, the diner is covered. I do get a day off every so often," I say with a wink. "Something you need to work on doing."

Margo scrunches up her nose. "I don't work on Sunday's. Well, I mean I go in to bake for the day, but Leanne does the rest."

I laugh, "Sweetness, having to wake up at three in the morning makes your 'day off' argument null and void. I mean a full day where you just laze in bed and do whatever it is that you want to do.

"What if what I want to do is bake?" she asks, her brow furrowed.

I drop a kiss to the top of her head as I hug her close. "Then, you bake."

She looks up at me with a wide smile. "What about staying in bed all day long with a sexy man?"

I can't hold in my possessive growl. "As long as that sexy man is me, then yes."

"That can be arranged," she says with a playful smirk.

The bells above the door ring, announcing yet another customer. I knew the bakery was busy, but it's busier than I ever knew. I turn to see who the intruder is and groan when I see Daisy. Not only is she a waitress at the diner, but she's my mother's best friend, which means everyone in town will know about Margo and me.

"Well, look who it is," Daisy teases.

"Mornin', Daisy," Margo says brightly, not caring that she just caught us making out with my hands on her curvy ass.

"Good mornin', darling. How are you this fine day?" she says, looking back and forth between Margo and me.

"I'm great. Thanks for asking," Margo answers with a huge smile. A smile that I'm hoping is more for me than Daisy. "How are you?"

"Better now," she replies with a smirk. She winks at me, and I groan. I know she's going to make a big deal out of what she saw. And if not her, my mom certainly will. I have zero doubt that as soon as Daisy leaves, the first thing that busybody will do is call my mom.

"Do you want your usual?" Margo asks, looking slightly confused by Daisy's response.

"Yes, please. And one of those fancy coffees you make."

"You bet."

It takes only a couple minutes and several meaningful looks between Daisy and me to get her muffins and coffee. Daisy pays, leaving an extra big tip in the jar, giving me another smile. "See you tomorrow, boss man."

"Bye, Daisy," I growl.

She leaves cackling the whole way.

"She's so sweet," Margo says. She's completely unaware of how quickly word of our interlude will blow up in the town. I hope she didn't want our relationship to be discreet because that just flew right out the window.

5

MARGO

IT'S BEEN TWO WEEKS. Two amazing weeks. Amos is everything I ever imagined he would be and so much more. I never thought we would find our way to each other. We danced around each other for a long time, and I never would have guessed that he wanted me as much as I wanted him. The girls were right about that, and I feel silly for ever doubting that.

My alarm goes off, and I stretch my deliciously sore body. Amos reaches across the bed and pulls me back against his chest. Oh, that's another thing, we haven't spent a single night without each other since that first night. We're either at his house or mine. We've settled into a routine that makes my heart soar.

"Come back here, sweetness," Amos growls in his sleep rough voice.

I protest half-heartedly like I do every morning when my alarm goes off but let him pull me close. I let out a cleansing breath. I love waking up with Amos. He never fails to give me extra cuddles... sometimes so much more. Again, zero complaints from me. Starting the day with a good orgasm is definitely a lovely boost of serotonin, better than any cup of coffee.

By the time I finally get out of bed, I'm running late. Before Amos, I hadn't been late a day in my life. I hate being late to anything no matter how trivial—though work is definitely not trivial—now that I'm with Amos, I can't find it in myself to feel anything other than happiness to run late. Even so, I rush through my morning routine. I'm only thirty minutes late when I get to Sprinkled With Sugar.

My phone dings with a text before I've even had time to turn and lock the door.

Amos. It's always him. *Lock the door, sweets.*

My heart flip flops in my chest. It never fails; every single morning, he texts to remind me to lock the door behind me. Something I hate to admit, but I'm really lax with doing. When he realized that I rarely if ever, lock up after I get here, he growled his caveman growl and told me that I needed to take better care with his woman.

It's locked, I reply.

Good. Need to make sure my girl is taking care of herself.

Swoon. I love it when he says stuff like that. Being Amos' girl is about the best thing in the whole world. With a lightness in my heart that's grown bigger and bigger every day, I start baking Sugarhill's favorite morning treats.

I've barely unlocked the doors when my first customer of the day strides in and straight to me. He pulls me into a hug and kisses me soundly. That's another thing that's changed. Amos is always my first customer. He comes and kisses me breathless, leaving me wet and needy, then he takes the diner's order and leaves with a smile... sometimes he whistles.

Both of us are stupid levels of happy. I chew on my lip when I think about how things are about to change. His parents are visiting for a week starting tomorrow. Tonight's the last night, I get to fall asleep and wake up in Amos' arms. He tells me I'm being ridiculous it won't matter to his parents if I'm there every night, but this trip is incredibly important to Amos and his family, and I don't want to be an interloper.

His dad's health is declining rapidly, and he has more bad days than good lately. He wanted to spend time in his hometown before he completely loses his mind to Alzheimer's. I'm extremely nervous about meeting them for the first time as Amos' girlfriend.

Of course, I've known them since my family moved here when I was in second grade, but this is different. Before I was just Margo Schultz, now I'm Margo Schultz, girlfriend to their only baby. Logically, I know his parents already like me... but what if they don't think I'm good enough for their son? That would be devastating.

My mood grows somber at that. When I told him my worries, he laughed it off and said I'm being ridiculous, that his parents already love me. He said his mom is over the moon that we are dating. Apparently, his mom has been trying to set him up for years, so she's thrilled.

I'm busy in Amo's kitchen, baking the infamous burnt sugar pie the entire town is in love with. Another thing I'm worried about, what if his parents are upset that Amos gave me the secret family recipe? I brush it off. Even though he told me I could start selling it in the bakery, I haven't. I refused vehemently. This is a Burnt Sugar Diner exclusive, and I refuse to mess with that. He thinks I'm being ridiculous, but I'm sticking to my guns on that one.

There's a brisk knock at the door, and heart starts pounding—time to meet the parents. Trudy, Amos' mother, wraps me up in a huge hug the moment she sees me. In fact, she completely bypasses her son to hug me. I look over Trudy's shoulder with a wide-eyed surprise at Amos.

He mouths, *"Told you so."*

And he did. All of my nerves slip away into her warm embrace. It's been a long time since I've had a mom hug. There's something special about mom hugs. My own mom and dad packed up to travel the world shortly after they retired. We talk often, but it's been almost a year since they've been home. Embarrassingly, my eyes burn with tears. Amos gives me a worried look, but I minutely shake my head, letting him know that everything is fine.

I'm shocked when his dad wraps me up in another hug. I never expected such a warm and enthusiastic greeting. All of my nervousness seems silly now. Dinner is great. Trudy and Alan regale me with stories of Amos as a boy and how much trouble he and my best friend's husband, Torin, got into. I can tell both Amos and Trudy are happy that Alan is having such a good day. He's completely lucid and happily talking about the past like it was just yesterday. I was warned that the days are rarely all good and to be prepared for his confusion.

The evening flies by, and before I know it, I'm hugging Trudy and Alan goodbye, and Amos is walking me out to my car.

"Are you sure you won't stay?" he asks grumpily.

"I don't want to give your parents the wrong idea about me. Right now, I'm the girlfriend. If I stay the night, that could change. What if your parents think I'm a hussy?"

He laughs at that. "First of all, who even says 'hussy' anymore?"

I stomp my foot and cross my arms over my chest. "Don't tease me!"

He pulls me into his arms, kissing the top of my head. "Sorry, sweets. I just hate not spending the night with you in my arms."

"Me too. I want to stay, I do, but I just can't risk your parents thinking less of me. I want them to like me... in case this thing blows up."

He growls at that. "Nothing is going to blow up with us unless you consider explosive orgasms blowing up, then yes, we'll be blowing up over and over."

I shiver at the reminder of how we are together. He's not wrong about the whole exploding thing. Every time is epic. Heck, it gets better with every time we have sex. Our chemistry is off the charts.

He opens my car door and kisses me so fiercely I'm panting by the time he pulls away. I know what he's doing. He's showing me exactly what I'm going to be missing by leaving. As if I don't already know.

"Text me when you get home, sweets."

It's easy to agree, even easier to give in to another kiss. My entire body is on fire with need as I pull out of his drive and head home. My house is empty and feels cold without Amos' presence in it. He's the kind of guy that fills up a space. Not obtrusively. It's just a feeling of security and a lack of aloneness. I miss him immediately and completely.

I take a lonely shower—something else that I rarely do anymore—and crawl under my blankets, alone. I sleep fitfully, missing Amos' warm weight against my back. It worries me a little that I'm so attached after only two weeks. We went from zero to one hundred, but it doesn't feel like it. Everything is so comfortable between us that it feels natural.

Waking up isn't any better than going to sleep alone. It doesn't help that I laid wide awake for hours. I feel a bit like a zombie. Coffee does nothing to wake me up. Somehow, I know that a dose of Amos will help wake me up, unlike my coffee. I grab all of my stuff and head into work.

My phone dings as soon as I get to the bakery. I smile, knowing it's going to be Amos telling me to lock up. My heart flutters when I read the message: *Lock up, sweetness. I miss you.*

I miss you too. I couldn't sleep without you.

I have an 'oh crap' moment when I realize what I just sent him, but then realize I don't care if it's too soon in our relationship to mention things like that. Not with Amos. He's not the type to freak out over feelings.

Likewise, love. I don't like being apart from you.

I thought I liked being his sweetness? Being his love? Wow. Yeah, that does something to me that I never thought I'd feel. Butterflies swarm my stomach, my heart is racing, and I'm smiling so wide my cheeks hurt. All the sleepiness disappears, and I'm floating on cloud nine.

No, he didn't say he loves me... but as far as I'm concerned, that's step one. I'm pretty sure I'm already on step three or four. Well, if there were steps to follow to get to such a strong emotion.

I'm so distracted that I burn two trays full of muffins and have to do them again. It's entirely unlike me to let anything distract me from my baking, but Amos is undoubtedly a worthy distraction if ever there were one.

"ARE you sure you don't mind?" I ask Leanne for the tenth time.

She rolls her eyes. "Margo, I've got this. I've been here for months. You can trust me to do one morning shift."

"Oh, honey, I do trust you. I just... it'll be the first morning since I opened that I'm not the one here."

Her eyes turn soft as understanding dawns on her. "I get it. It's hard to let go a little when something is so important to you. I promise everything will be fine. Go enjoy the morning with your boyfriend and his parents. That's way more important than giving Mr. Phizer his black coffee and bran muffins."

We both laugh at that. I make those muffins just for him. He comes every Saturday to pick up the entire dozen. It's the most boring thing that I make. I mean, they are delicious because I don't bake anything that doesn't have a little pizazz, but they are definitely not the strawberry cream cheese muffins or the triple chocolate chunk muffins that taste like sin.

"Okay, well, if you need anything, just call..."

"Go!" Leanne says, waving me away. "I swear I'll be fine. Sprinkled With Sugar will run just fine without you for a morning."

IT FEELS weird to knock on Amos' door... I have a key— another thing that was probably way too early in our relationship to do based on other peoples' standards but feels perfect for us. Amos opens the door a moment later with a confused expression. Probably wondering why I didn't just let myself in.

"Did you forget your key?"

I shake my head. "I didn't know if you would want your parents to know that we are basically living at each other's houses and that we exchanged keys. That's a big step..."

Amos pulls me into his arms and gives me the kiss to end all kisses. "Love, I want the world to know that we are at the almost living together stage."

"I-" I have no idea what I was about to say when his mom comes to the door and slaps Amos' arm and tells him to let me inside.

Trudy pulls me inside and gives me a tight squeeze. "So glad you could make it. I made pancakes."

I give her a happy smile as Amos puts his hand on my lower back and leads me to the table. Alan is already there, eating his pancakes with a big glass of orange juice.

"Good morning, Alan," I say with a smile.

The whole feeling in the room turns darker, and I have to wonder if he's having a bad day, and I shouldn't greet him in case seeing a new face will confuse him.

"Margo! I'm so happy to see you. Amos sure did marry a pretty one, don't you think, Tru?"

I blink at Alan and open my mouth to respond, but Amos steps in before I can say anything. "I'm a lucky man, that's for sure."

I look back at Amos, and he's got a troubled but determined look on his face. Obviously, Alan is having a bad day and is confused. I'm not sure why no one isn't correcting him, but I don't want to be the one to upset him, so I choose to not say anything either.

"Sit, sit! Let's eat," he says boisterously, having no idea the bomb of a mess he just dropped.

Except... some part of me is thrilled at the thought of being married to Amos. Did I say zero to a hundred? Make that zero to a thousand. I'm not upset about the idea of being married. I'm upset because Alan is such a sweetheart, and is this is evidence of how bad his dementia is getting. I feel horrible for Trudy and Amos... Alan too. I can't imagine what it's like to lose a loved one in this way, nor can I imagine the frustration of losing your memories.

We all sit down and eat breakfast, the mood somber.

I spend the whole day with them, going on a drive around the town so that Alan can see all the things. We stop into the bakery, and he gets one of my mini apple pies, which he declares to be better than any pie he's ever had. Trudy seems to get offended because the burnt sugar pie recipe is something from her family, but then she winks at me, and I know she's just teasing him. They have such a sweet relationship. They are constantly touching and teasing each other. They radiate love and affection. It's exactly the kind of marriage I want one of these days.

We eat dinner at the diner, and Alan seems to regain himself at the familiar surroundings... except for one thing... he still thinks I'm married to Amos.

Because of Alan's confusion, Amos talks me into staying the night. He doesn't want to make things worse, and I can't argue with his logic.

"I can't believe you're just letting him believe we are married!" I whisper-shout when we are safely behind closed doors and out of earshot of his parents. "Seriously, Amos. That's... it's... crazy!"

"I'm sorry," he apologizes, taking me in his arms. "I just... My dad..."

He looks and sounds so sad any anger I had melts away, and I hug him tight. "It's okay. I mean, it's not a hardship being fake married. You're right that it means I can stay here without your parents thinking I'm a hussy."

He chuckles. "Hussy..."

I slap his chest. "Don't make fun of me. I'm your wife. You're supposed to be nice to me."

"Sorry, wifey. Forgive me?"

My heart skips a beat then beats out of control at hearing Amos call me his wife. Okay, I am totally screwed. This is fake, I remind myself. Fake. We aren't married, heck we aren't even engaged. We're dating.

"How can I stay mad at you, hubby?" I ask, tilting my head back for a kiss.

6

With a growl, I lean down and kiss my pretend wife. Though thinking the word pretend feels wrong. I want to be her husband in truth, which is something that smacked me in the face when my dad mentioned it. The caveman inside me wanted nothing more than to beat his chest and drag Margo off to the nearest court-house to make it real.

I fist her wild curls in my hand and deepen the kiss. Completely owning her lips, her tongue, all of her. She groans when I tighten my fist in her hair. My girl likes it a little rough, something that I'm more than happy to oblige.

"Amos," she breathes between kisses, "please. I need you."

I nip her chin then neck, kissing away the sting. "And you'll have me soon."

"Now," she whimpers, threading her hands in my hair as I kiss down her neck to the top of her shirt. I pull the shirt over her head and toss it to the floor. I take a second to admire her pretty blue bra, knowing she picked it with me in mind makes my cock even harder. Then I strip her of it too. Her dusky pink nipples are diamond points begging for my mouth. It would be a sin to ignore them, so my mouth wraps around the first one, then the other. I flick them with my tongue, sucking and nibbling on them until Margo's knees buckle from pleasure.

"Please," she whimpers.

I slowly finish undressing her, then myself, loving the slow tease and the heated way she's looking at me. I pick her up and toss her onto the bed, then descend on her pussy with one purpose and one purpose only—to make my girl come all over my mouth so I can drink her down.

"Oh, God!" she cries out when I suck her sensitive clit, letting the sharp edge of my teeth lightly rake over it just like she likes. Her back arches as moans, "I'm going to come. Don't stop... don't stop... Oh God..." And then she's exploding for me. I lick up her release, teasing her to another orgasm. She collapses back to the bed for a moment, and I crawl up her body, kissing her soft skin as I go until I'm devouring her lips again.

I reach for a condom on the nightstand, but she grabs my hand and shakes her head. "I want to feel you... all of you," she says with a naughty glint in her eye. "I want you to come deep inside me. I want to feel you pulsing and emptying into me."

I give her a questioning look.

"I'm on the pill," she clarifies. A little jolt of disappointment burns in my gut, which is ridiculous. It's too soon to think babies. "And I'm clean."

I kiss her fiercely. "I'm clean too."

Unable to control myself at the thought of rutting into her bare, I thrust into her hard and fast. She lets out a scream, that I dampen with another kiss, lest my parents hear her. I'm harder than ever before. Fucking her like a madman as she screams into the pillow, biting down to keep her screams muffled.

She says something that sounds sort of like "I'm gonna come," but it's muffled.

Her nails scratch down my chest as her pussy clenches around my cock, choking the life out of it as she comes. Her pussy gripping me so tight, pulls me right over the edge with her. I bury myself deep and let go, filling her with rope after sticky rope of my release.

I collapse next to her, pulling her into my arms and kissing her slow and sweet. I run my hands over her body, unable to stop touching her. I dip my fingers between her wet, and swollen pussy lips where my come is slowly dripping from her tight channel and rub my come up and over her clit. I slowly stroke her clit in small circles until her hips are moving into my touch, and she's moaning lowly. Before she can tip over into an orgasm, I pull her on top of me and set her on my cock.

She moans, rubbing herself along the underside of my cock. Seeing the way her pussy lips are spread around me, as she rubs our releases all over me is so lude, I could come just from the sight of my cock peeking out as she rubs along me. Unable to take another minute, I grip her hips and slowly guide her onto me. She lowers herself until my cock is buried to the hilt. She throws her head back, moaning.

"God, you're so deep this way. Hurts so good," Margo groans as she starts moving.

Slowly she rises and falls on my cock, her hips dancing up and down as she finds her perfect rhythm, one that will send us both over the edge to oblivion. I take one of her nipples in my mouth, teasing it with my tongue. The other gets the same adoring treatment. She lowers her mouth to mine, and we kiss in slow, languid caresses of our tongues. Her hips never quit their perfect dance. This isn't the passionate fucking from last time. This is something more. Something that says all the words neither of us has been brave enough to say yet, but I'm sure both of us feel.

I slip my fingers between us, finding her clit and gently rubbing. She raises up, throwing her head back as she moves a bit faster. Rolling her hips and falling on my cock harder. It doesn't take long for her to come on a scream that she barely muffles with her hand. Her inhibitions are completely gone leaving nothing but the wanton beauty riding me to my own release. She buries me deep inside the hot clench of her pussy and squeezes down as her orgasm rips through her body. My balls draw up, and then I'm coming with her, once again flooding her pussy with my come until its overflowing.

Margo collapses onto my chest, breathing heavily. "We're really, really good at that. Not bad for a fake relationship," she mumbles sleepily.

My mood instantly sours. I hate the sound of us

being fake in any way. I hope like hell she understands that letting my dad think we are married is the only fake thing in our relationship. We are very much real, and we are very much moving towards something more permanent.

I'm awake late into the night, my thoughts troubled. Eventually, I fall asleep wrapped around Margo as she sleeps soundly. It seems like I've barely closed my eyes when her alarm goes off. She quietly gets up in hopes of not waking me up. I watch as she silently moves about the room, getting dressed for the day. When she's done, I stand from the bed and wrap her up in my arms, holding her tight.

Margo clings to me in a way that tells me something is wrong, but now isn't the time to discuss things with her. We don't have time to have that kind of conversation. I walk her to the door and kiss her goodbye. I can't stop the worry that bubbles up, wondering if I somehow messed things up with her last night. This morning she welcomed my embrace easily enough, but something was off. Almost like she was closed off to me... pulling away emotionally.

I shake my head. Surely, I'm making more of this than there is. She's probably just tired. Once again, I kept her up later than her usual bedtime making love to her for hours. There's no going back to sleep after seeing off to work, so I decide to go for a run to clear my head.

I'm fresh out of the shower and drinking my first cup of coffee of the morning when my parents come down for breakfast. I whip up some frittatas and bacon the whole time I'm cooking, wondering if my dad will be himself today or if another piece of his mind will be gone.

"This is wonderful, son," my dad says, wiping his mouth with his napkin. "Your talents really are wasted at that diner. Daisy says you haven't changed the menu at all since you've taken over. You're a trained chef... you should be cooking things like this."

I shrug, "I love working at the diner. I love giving folks what they want."

Dad shakes his head. "They don't know if they want your fancy breakfasts if you don't try. You should add some specials and see how they do. I think you'll be surprised."

"Maybe," I say to appease him, though I have no intentions of changing his menu. I get my love of cooking from him, and changing the menu feels like another small loss of his memory.

"I have something for you," my dad says, pulling a small wooden box from under the table.

I know exactly what's in that box, and my heart starts to pound. He hands over the box that holds my great-great-grandmother's wedding ring. My parents were already married when my grandmother passed on, and the ring was left to my father. He was supposed to keep it until it was time for me to get married. Why is he giving it to me now?

"I know it's not the way it's traditionally done, but it's time. I want you to have this before my mind is completely stolen away from me. I'd love to see that ring used before it happens, but seeing it in your hands makes me happy enough.

Maybe it's about time for you to use it already on that pretty little baker of yours. It would be nice to see my only son married off and happy before..." he sighs sadly.

"It's okay, dad. Thank you for this," I say, fisting the box tight in my hand, the pointed corners biting into my palm. I should be thankful that my dad is one hundred percent himself today, but that means there's no need for Margo to be my fake wife.

Why does that upset me so badly?

MARGO

"Margo!" Lani says as she throws her arms around me. "It feels like it's been ages!"

I laugh. "It's been five days."

She shakes her head. "Like I said, ages."

Prue rolls her eyes. "She's so dramatic now that she's all knocked up."

We all laugh at that because she's not wrong.

Ana is the next to hug me. "Hey hon, is everything okay? You look troubled."

Leave it to Ana to see something behind my smiles. She's way to perceptive for her own good. Definitely works against all of us when we try to hide something.

"I'm okay... it's just..." I hesitate to say anything because the whole fake marriage thing seems not only ridiculous, but I want it to be real, and that right there is ridiculous.

"Spit it out already," Prue says with a roll of her eyes. She's never one to beat around the bush and hates when others do too.

"You all know that Amos' dad has Alzheimer's, right?" They all nod. "Well, yesterday was an off day, and he confused me for Amos' wife. I went to correct him, but Amos stepped in and agreed with him. Can you believe it?!

"So now I'm fake married to Amos, who I've been dating officially for only two weeks. It's... ridiculous."

"And yet you seem sad that it's fake," Ana says.

Once again, my friend is way too perceptive. I distract everyone from the conversation by handing out everyone's favorite treats. We move to the small table I have set up for the random customers that like to eat here instead of taking their desserts and leaving.

"I've known Amos for a long time," Ana starts. "He's not one to do anything he doesn't want to do."

I shake my head, "Except he would do anything for his father. Including lying to protect him from feeling like he's crazy."

"Except that..." she agrees. "Even so, I don't think that's a lie he would let stand if he wasn't already thinking about the future of your relationship and where he wants it to go."

"I love weddings," Lani adds around a big bite of muffin. "They are my favorite. Watching two people vow themselves to each other..."

It's my turn to roll my eyes. "What part of fake did you not understand? This isn't real, Lani. Amos didn't propose. This whole relationship is fake."

Ana purses her lips. "Not the whole relationship, just the married part. Amos is completely smitten with you—probably even in love with you."

My eyes go wide at that. No way is he in love with me after two weeks. Guys don't fall that quick, not like women. I mean, I know I'm in love with the big gruff diner owner who treats me like a queen, but he's not there. Yes, he likes me a lot... love? No way.

"Ana is right," Prue adds. "That man has been gone for you for months."

After a lot of back and forth where my friends almost have me convinced that Amos is in love with me even though he hasn't said anything of the sort yet, I'm more confused than ever when they leave.

Thankfully Leanne comes in shortly after, and I'm able to leave her in charge while I escape to my house. I need time to myself. Time to think and to talk myself out of the craziness my friends tried to pollute my mind with.

They're wrong. This whole thing is fake. Yes, we exchanged keys and are dating seriously, but this marriage is fake, and thinking that he wants it to be real is ridiculous. It's off the rails levels of crazy. I take a hot shower and have myself firmly back on solid ground by the time I'm done getting ready for the evening.

My phone dings with a text from Amos asking me when I'll be home. My heart skips a beat or three at the question. I know he's not talking about my house. He wants to know when I will be home to his.

Home.

When did Amos' house become home? Jesus, I'm in deeper than I ever thought. I text him that I'll be there soon. I can't hide out forever.

I LET myself into his house this time, knowing that someone who is married to the homeowner wouldn't feel the need to knock. Trudy seems genuinely excited to see me and throws her arms around me in one of those perfect mom hugs that I've missed so badly since my parents moved.

Alan is the next to hug me. Then it's Amos. I feel like I collapse into his embrace. Not my body, but my heart. He gives me a gentle smile and a sweet kiss that he deepens until it's barely appropriate to be seen by his parents.

"I've missed you," he says for my ears only.

"Me too," I confess. It's true. I did miss him. I miss him every time we're apart for any length of time.

During dinner, it becomes apparent that Alan is completely himself. A small piece of me is disappointed. My friends' encouragement at the whole 'Amos wouldn't do anything unless he really wanted to' thing is screwing with my mind.

"So, tell me, Margo, do you want children?"

I nearly choke on my water at the question. "I... uh... someday, yes." I look at Amos with wide eyes, always shocked by the things that come out of Alan's mouth. Though tonight he's completely lucid. "I would have to find the right man and be married before even thinking about that."

Trudy purses her lips and looks between Amos and me in one of those meaningful kind of ways. Like she sees everything and knows that our relationship is much more than it is.

"Hopefully, Amos will settle down soon. I'd like to meet my grandchildren before..." he trails off.

We all know what before he's talking about. The entire mood shifts to a somber one. He wants grandkids before he loses the ability to know them. Even if he won't remember them once he loses himself to his disease completely.

I'm getting ready to leave for the night when Amos asks me to stay. He uses the excuse that he wants me here in case his father wakes up confused again, but I can read him better than that. He's feeling insecure in the same way that I am and wants to keep me close. I don't put up even the pretense of an argument.

THE NEXT MORNING Alan seems to be himself but also seems sad. Trudy says he gets that way sometimes, but that he's fine. We end up having dinner at the diner so his dad can check that off the list of things he wants to do during their week-long vacation.

The diner is busy like it always is on Sunday night, and we quickly claim the only table left. I'm happy to see it's in Ana's section. Her smile is strained when she greets us and asks what we'd like to eat. Alan and Trudy order burgers, and I get my usual—chicken-fried steak and baked potato. Amos gets the special.

I want to ask my friend what's wrong but now isn't the time. It doesn't take long to figure out the problem:

Carson Moore. He's got a serious thing for Ana. He's constantly flirting in this way over the top way that makes sweet, innocent Ana uncomfortable. I make a note to mention it to Amos and see if there's anything he can do.

"Margo, where is your ring?" Alan asks, seeming panicked. "You didn't lose it, did you?"

I cover my left hand, feeling guilty because he's obviously slipped back into his delusions. I can't hide my panic because there is no ring. How do I explain this one away? Turns out, I don't have to because Amos produces a gorgeous ring from his pocket.

"I almost forgot, sweetness. You left this beside the sink this morning." I'm completely gobsmacked with the fact that he's carrying around a wedding ring. A freakin' beautiful one at that. It's classic and simple, but the diamond is enormous. I try to figure out if the ring is a fake that he got in case his dad needs it.

It has to be a fake, right?

"Oh goodness! I'm so glad you found it," I say, once again playing along with Alan's delusion even though I hate the lie.

When Ana comes to collect the plates, she notices the ring, and her eyes go wide. I nod towards the bathroom, and she gives her own imperceptible nod.

"Excuse me." I get up from the table and bolt—slowly and with dignity—to the bathroom.

Ana is already there. She grabs my hand first thing and looks between the rock on my finger and me. "What is that?!"

I shake my head, letting her know without words

that it's fake. "His dad is confused again... he asked where my ring is like it's something important, and then Amos pulled this out of his pocket. Next thing I know, I'm wearing this wedding ring!"

"Wow."

"I know! I'm kind of freaking out here, Ana. A ring doesn't feel like we are fake married. It feels like we've upped the ante or something."

Ana hugs me. "It's okay. Don't panic. I'm sure he was just carrying it to be prepared for if his dad ever asked. If he meant it to be more than that, he would've proposed for real. Amos doesn't do anything half-assed."

I nod, trying to calm my racing heart. "You're right. This is just a ring. A piece of the illusion we are providing for Alan."

"See, no need to panic. At least, not until you have a chance to talk to Amos."

I find myself nodding again—I'm doing that a lot lately. "I saw you talking to Carson..."

Ana blows a loose hair out of her face, a look of consternation on her face. "He's impossible. One minute he's a jerk telling me my skirt is too short, the next he's flirting like crazy, then he's back to being a jerk. I hate him."

"I think he likes you. Why else would he constantly sit in your section, and even when he can't demand that you serve his table?"

She snorts, "If he liked me, he wouldn't be such a dick to me. I think he just likes to screw with me."

"Amos was all gruff and growly with me for months before we started dating…"

She gives me a dirty look that I know she doesn't really mean. "That was different. Amos is just gruff and overprotective growly, and he was constantly looking for ways to be around you."

I raise my brow. "Exactly."

Ana huffs. "Not the same."

"Whatever you say," I laugh. "We better get back out there before someone comes looking for us."

Once I'm back at the table, Amos asks if everything is okay. I give him the brightest, fakest smile I can muster because I have zero idea how to answer that question without a mild freak out. Definitely not something I want to do in public and especially not in front of his parents.

Amos and I are getting ready for bed when he pulls me into his arms. "Sweetness, are you okay?"

I close my eyes and relax into his arms. "I don't know," I say honestly. "I know all this is fake," I wiggle my fingers, so he knows what I'm talking about, "but sometimes it… I don't know."

"Feels real?" he finishes.

I bury my face in his chest and nod my head. I am so ashamed of my feelings, especially since I know this isn't real. This is all part of keeping Alan happy and letting him believe that Amos is married and happy.

"It's just ridiculous, isn't it?" I feel vulnerable as I ask.

He shakes his head. "No… not at all, love. There are

moments like this one that everything feels right and real."

Tell me you want it to be real, my heart silently begs.

"But it's not. Just like this ring."

Amos tugs me down onto his lap as he sits on the bed. "This ring is very real. My dad brought it to give to me before his mind completely betrays him. This was my great-great-grandmother's wedding ring.

"Wait, what?! You gave me a family heirloom to wear?" I start pulling the ring off my finger to give it back to him. Only the woman he plans to marry in truth should ever wear anything as special as this.

He grabs my hand, preventing me from taking it off, and kisses my finger above the ring. "It looks good on you."

My heart leaps. This moment feels very real. It is fraught with emotions that I didn't realize I was ready for. I want to marry Amos. It's official, I'm insane. I've flown right over the cuckoo's nest.

"Besides, you need to keep it in case my dad asks again."

And then I'm knocked straight off of cloud nine, and I'm brought straight back to reality.

8

Seeing my grandmother's ring on Margo's finger is like a punch in the gut. I wasn't lying when I said it looks good on her. I love how it looks, but the panicked look on her face when I told her it was a family heirloom was enough to have me holding back, telling her my true feelings.

The reality is that I love Margo Schultz, and I want to make her mine forever. The only problem is I don't want her to think I'm telling her this because of my father. He's told her how much he wants me happy and with kids before he's completely gone... I don't want to make her feel pressured or like she's just the convenient option.

That's not it at all.

It's all about loving her and wanting to spend my life with her in my arms. Now to just find a way to keep her...

"I think you should move in." I find myself saying without actually thinking it through.

Margo looks at me with a furrowed brow and an almost hopeful light in her eyes. The first sign that she might actually want the same things I want. "You mean until your parents leave?"

I shrug, "That's a start." I'll have to do whatever I can to convince her to stay long after this fake marriage for my dad's sake is over... like forever. I want that ring on her finger in truth, not just this farce.

———

I HATE that I have to spend the day at work when my parents are here. Thankfully, Margo has Leanne covering for her at the bakery, so she's taking my parents to Clearwater to visit with my father's sister for the day.

There's a brisk knock on the door before it swings open and a very flustered Ana storms into my office. "I can't do this anymore!" she shouts, throwing her arms in the air. "That man is impossible. He's a jackass, and I just can't."

"Carson?" I ask even though I know exactly who she's talking about. Carson owns Sweet Rides, the only repair shop in town, though he specializes in customizing Harleys. And he is utterly obsessed with Analise, the sweetest person in all of Sugarhill. She doesn't have a mean bone in her body. The fact that she is in here yelling and cursing say she's finally fed up with him.

"Of course," she flails her arms again, "Can you ban him from coming here? He refuses to leave me alone."

"Has he touched you?" I ask with a low growl.

"No, nothing like that. He just won't let anyone else serve him and then acts like a jerk to me. Tells me my skirts are too short or my jeans are too tight. Today he doesn't like my shirt!"

"Then I can't exactly ban him."

"But it's harassment! Can you at least make him sit in someone else's section? Please, Amos. I can't take this anymore." Ana's eyes become glassy, and I swear she might cry. That is unacceptable. I didn't realize how much Carson actually upset her.

"Okay. I'll talk to him." Not that it will do a bit of good. I know exactly what it looks like when a man has staked his claim on a woman, and Carson has most definitely staked his claim. Ana doesn't realize it, but he's acting out of jealousy and protectiveness. It's only a matter of time until he makes his move.

Ana lets out a relieved sigh. "Thank you, Amos."

"Anytime."

It's late when I get home. My parents are in bed already, and Margo is asleep on the couch. I pick her up and carry her to our room. She sleepily nuzzles my chest. "You're home."

I kiss the top of her head. "I am. Sorry I'm so late."

"Missed you," she murmurs.

I put her in bed then strip so I can crawl in beside her. She turns and curls up against me, her head on my chest. With a sleepy sigh, she falls right back asleep.

TRUDY AND ALAN are leaving today. They are cutting their trip short because Alan has had several bad days in a row, and Trudy is worried it's because he's not around familiar things. Being at home can help remind him of who he is and who she is when he sees the pictures on the wall and the notes they have all over their condo to remind him of other things he might forget.

Amos is upset but understands their reasoning for leaving. I'm disappointed myself. Not just because that means the fake marriage and temporary living situation is changing. I genuinely love his parents. Trudy and Alan have welcomed me into the family like I've been a part of them forever. It's been nice, but it makes me miss my own parents. It's a stark reminder that I need to make more of an effort to talk to them... maybe even take the time to meet them on one of their many adventures.

It's late by the time we get home from driving them

to the city so they can catch their flight. I can't stop yawning, and at one point, doze off. We get back to Amos' house, and the sadness of leaving and heading back to my house hits me.

"I guess I'll head home. I need to get some sleep. I'll come get my stuff tomorrow if that's okay?" I say, taking off his great-great-grandmother's ring and handing it back.

Amos hesitates to take the ring back. For a split second, I think he's going to protest and put the ring right back on my finger, but he pockets it instead. "Why don't you stay tonight? You're tired, you shouldn't be driving even if it is only a few minutes away."

I don't put up much of a fight because staying is exactly what I want to do. I don't ever want to go home to an empty house again. I want to stay here. As soon as we get into bed with each other, all of my tiredness flees at the feel of his skin on mine.

I roll so that I'm draped over his chest. In less than a blink of an eye, Amos has his lips on mine in a drugging kiss. He grabs my ass and lifts me until I'm straddling his waist, my panties, and his boxers the only barriers between us. He lifts my shirt over my head and tosses it away. His hands run down my body, caressing my back, my ass, then up my sides to my breasts. I moan as he lightly pinches my nipples.

His hands go back to my hips, and he pulls me down tighter against him, pushing me up and back across his cock. We both groan at the movement. His cock drags across my clit, and my core clenches. I gasp when he rolls us, so I'm flat on my back.

"You're so fucking beautiful, Margo," he says, kissing his way down my body. "I love these curves of yours." He gently nips the underside of my breast before kissing the small hurt better. He circles my nipple with his tongue, teasing it into a stiff peak. Then does the same to the other. I thread my fingers through his hair, holding him to me, begging him not to stop the delicious torture.

His fingers trail down to the apex of my thighs. He grips my lacy panties and pulls them tight. The next thing I hear is the sound of rendering fabric and a low growl as Amos' fingers find my soaking slit. My hips jerk when he zeroes in on my clit, circling it in quick, sure strokes. My orgasm comes hard and fast, completely stealing the breath from my lungs.

He gives me no time to catch my breath before he's got his face buried in my pussy, licking up my release. He fucks me with his tongue then moves up to lick my sensitive clit. I nearly jump off the bed when he thrusts two thick fingers into me, hitting my g-spot over and over until I'm coming completely undone.

"Amos! Oh, God... fuck..."

"That's it, sweetness, come all over my mouth."

The vibrations of his words against my pussy pushes me over the edge into oblivion. Stars explode behind my eyes, and I nearly faint from the force of the orgasm. I've barely caught my breath when Amos pushes inside me. I expect him to fuck me hard and fast after that, but he doesn't.

He pushes into me one inch at a time, dragging it out into one slow, smooth motion. He moves with such slow precision as he looks into my eyes. His look is so intense and screams of untold emotions. I wonder if he can see the love echoed back at him in mine?

We find our releases together, coming as we look into each other's eyes. Tears form in mine at the intimacy. I've never experienced something so overwhelming and perfect in my life.

"Move in with me, Margo. I don't want you here temporarily. That will never be enough."

My heart screams *'yes, yes, yes!'* but my mind says I should think about it at least a little... my heart wins, and I practically shout my yes. I'm so excited and happy that he wants me and not just as a temporary thing to appease his father.

We make love for the rest of the night. He takes me over and over again, making sweet love to me each time. Several times I nearly tell him how much I love him, but I bite my tongue. Moving in together has to be enough... for now.

10

"HOW DO you have so much shit?" Prue complains as she carries another box from the moving truck into Amos' garage... well, my garage. A little thrill shoots through me at the reminder that I'm moving in with him—today!

"Lani, put that fucking box down right now!" Torin yells from across the yard.

She gives him the finger over her back as she carries the small box of yarn from my failed attempts at learning to crochet. "I mean, that man would bitch about me lifting a pillow right now."

"I think it's sweet," Ana says with a sigh. She's always been a romantic. I've seen the way she looks at Torin and Lani... even me and Amos... she gets this dreamy, almost sad expression.

It takes an hour to unload the truck full of boxes. Most of my furniture was donated to Goodwill. The garage is full, and it's a little overwhelming, but I look forward to merging my things with Amos'.

I hug the girls, and they all head off to Lani's book-store for "book club." I opted out of today's club because I want to get a head start on unpacking. I'm just getting ready to grab the first box when I hear Amos and Torin talking just outside.

"It's insane... the whole marriage thing. All of this is crazy," Amos says. "I must be insane..."

Tears instantly well up in my eyes. I don't stick around to hear what else he says. I can't. I drop the box I'm holding and rush to the bathroom. I barely get the door closed before the tears start falling. My heart breaking into a million pieces.

Yes, I know our brief "marriage" was a sham, but Amos didn't seem to think it was ridiculous at the time. He even mentioned several times how good his grand-mother's ring looked on me. Does he just not want to get married? Or does he just not want to marry me? If that's the case and marrying me is ridiculous, why would he have me move in? Yeah, we haven't said 'I love you,' yet, but the sentiment has been there in the way we make love. The way we touch. All the little things we do, the I love you is unspoken but there in dozens of ways.

He's been showing me how he feels from the start. Did I completely read him wrong all these weeks? I thought I knew what he's feeling... maybe I've been very mistaken.

Once I hear Torin leave, I emerge from the bath-room feeling wrung dry. Amos seems over the moon happy when he tugs me against his chest and kisses me. I hardly hold myself together but manage to return his kiss, if a little less enthusiastically than usual. He gives me a confused look when he pulls away as if he knows something is wrong but can't put his finger on what.

"I need to go to the bakery. I completely forgot about a huge order that I need to get a jump start on," I say, making up a loosely veiled excuse to leave.

"I can come help," Amos offers with a happy smile.

I quickly shake my head. "No, I've got it."

My words come out harsher than I meant them to. He looks hurt and confused by my rejection. Maybe I imagined the conversation with Torin because he's not acting like a man who thinks this whole thing is ridiculous. But no, I know exactly what I heard. I also know that I need to be alone right now to work through my emotional rollercoaster.

THE BAKERY IS dark and quiet, exactly what I need to get my head on straight. There isn't any order to prep for. I feel slightly guilty for the white lie, but then I remember Amos' words, and the guilt disappears. He's been lying to me by omission this whole time. I know two wrongs don't make a right, but this is about self-preservation at this point.

I decide to go ahead and start baking for the day. I begin with bread. I could definitely use a little physical release in the form of kneading the heck out of some dough. By the time the bread is in the oven, I don't feel any better. My heart is still raw, and my eyes burn from the hundreds of tears I've shed. I pull myself up on the counter and open the container of leftover cookies from yesterday and start eating.

Even though I know they are delicious, the cookies taste like cardboard in my mouth. It's not fair. Heartache is supposed to make all food taste good. That's why binge eating is a thing after breakups, right? Not that I would know. This is my first time experiencing this level of hurt.

At midnight my phone starts ringing. Of course it's Amos. He's probably calling to see when I'll be home. Which brings on another wave of worry. I gave up my rental house when I agreed to move in with him. If things are over with Amos, where will I stay?

If we can't work past whatever this is and I decide to move right back out, then I'm essentially homeless. That has tears welling up again, but this time I sniff them back. Crying isn't helping anything. The real question is if he feels like marriage is ridiculous, can I live with him? Should I stay and hope he changes his mind?

I've always wanted marriage, babies, the whole happily ever after thing. Can I just put my hopes on him changing his mind in the future? Can I give up my dreams of forever for something that's a for now?

No, I don't think I can.

A few minutes later, my text alert dings. Without looking, I'm sure it's Amos again. I'm still not ready to talk to him, so I ignore the dings and go back to baking.

Time to make cupcakes. Three hours later, I have six dozen cupcakes—way more than I'll ever sell in one day. Oh well, this wasn't about stocking my shelves. This is my therapy. Once again, I perch myself on the counter, only this time, I have a triple chocolate strawberry cream-filled cupcake—a new recipe born of sadness but tastes like happiness. I eat two cupcakes before I dare to look at my phone.

It's almost two in the morning, and I have a ton of missed calls and texts from Amos. With the level of concern in his texts, I'm surprised he didn't just show up here to see me with his own eyes. Apparently, he got the message that I want to be left alone even if he doesn't understand why.

I read through the texts that start with his usual 'lock the door' and go through to 'I miss you, sweetness. Our bed is cold without you.' That last text came in ten minutes ago.

I'm flooded with feelings of guilt at making him worry. I hit reply and can't think of anything to say.

I'm fine, is what I finally settle on. Lame.

Three dots start bouncing almost instantly. *Are you sure, sweetness? You've never stayed out like this...*

I let out a troubled sigh. This isn't a conversation that should be done via text. It would make it so easy, but that's a cop-out, and I know it. *Yeah, everything is fine. I'm just going to stay and finish up today's baking since it's almost time for me to come in anyway.*

Amos doesn't respond. I don't know why, but tears prick my eyes again at how easily he accepted my excuse. I ignore the pang in my chest and start making things that actually fill my cases for the day.

Fifteen minutes later, there is a knock on the back-door. "Margo, open up," Amos shouts through the heavy metal door.

I stand frozen, staring at the door as if it's a cobra ready to strike.

11

AMOS

IT'S BEEN HOURS, and Margo hasn't answered her phone nor any of the dozens of text messages I've sent. It takes all of my self-control to not crash into the bakery like a madman. I do drive past twice just to make sure her car is there. I have to know she's safe even if she's not telling me herself.

Finally, at nearly two in the morning, she responds, telling me she's fine. I instinctively know that she's using the universal "I'm not at all fine" kind of fine. That's the last straw. I grab my keys and am out the door and heading through the night to Sprinkled With Sugar to see what's wrong with my girl.

Maybe she's just panicking about moving in? Our relationship has happened very quickly, but I thought we were both on the same page. I'm starting to regret not shouting from the rooftops that I love her. Could moving in cause added confusion about where we stand?

I'm not sure how she could mistake any part of our

relationship as anything but love. I might not have said the words, but I've shown her in every way possible. I love her more than anything. She's my entire world. I'm going to marry that woman.

I knock on the door and shout for Margo to open up. A few seconds later, I hear the lock disengage. My girl is there looking beautiful even though she's covered in flour and has obviously been crying. She lets me inside and then shuts and locks the door. I look around the kitchen, and it's an absolute wreck. It's then I know for sure something is really wrong. Margo is meticulous with her kitchen. She works clean and seamlessly moves from project to project.

Before she can walk away from me, I grab her up in a fierce hug. She's stiff in my arms, but I don't let go. Ever so slowly, she starts to relax into me. I kiss the top of her head, just holding her. Offering her comfort from whatever it is that's upset her.

"What's wrong, sweetness?"

She buries her face in my shirt and shakes her head, refusing to answer.

"How can I fix this if you won't talk to me?"

"I heard you," she says with a whimper.

I pull away to look down at her upturned face. "What did you hear?"

"You told Torin this thing was all ridiculous," she sniffles.

"Oh, baby, no. That's... no. *Nothing* about us is ridiculous. Not a single thing. I love you, Margo. I was asking Torin if *I* was ridiculous for wanting to do this..." I say, kneeling on the flour-covered floor and taking the ring out of my pocket. "Marry me, Margo Schultz, make me the luckiest man alive."

She blinks down at me in wide-eyed shock. For a brief moment, I feel anxious that I was right, thinking this is ridiculously fast. It feels right, though. Margo stares at me for what feels like an eternity, tears welling in her beautiful green eyes, then she throws herself at me, knocking us both to the floor.

"Yes!" she cries. "Yes, Amos, I want to be your wife. I love you so much. I was so worried that you didn't feel this crazy fast love like I did. I assumed the worst. I should've talked to you, but I was just so scared."

I pull her in for a kiss, silencing her. She kisses me back, enthusiastically. I'm so lost in our kisses and touches that I'm not exactly sure how it happens, but we are both naked, and she's got her lips wrapped tight around my hard cock. She sucks me deep, choking a little at my length. Her little fist moves up and down, the strokes feel like heaven, but not nearly as good as her mouth.

She's working my cock like she wants my come. I grip her hair tight, thrusting up into her mouth, unable to control myself. My balls draw up tight, and I can feel my come begging to be released. I pull her away before I lose it. She gasps and whimpers, sticking her tongue out to lick the drop of precome from my tip.

"I'm coming in that sweet little pussy of yours," I growl.

She moans, crawling up my body with bright, excited eyes. My eyes nearly cross when she rubs her wet slit over my cock, spreading her sweet honey all over me. That's not what I want either. I want her to come all over my face. I want to drink her down.

I grab her hips and lift her, placing her down right on my face. "Ride my face, sweets. Ride my face and give me that cream."

"I've never... I'm too..."

I slap my hand on her ass before she can make a comment about being too big. It's utter bullshit. I love her curves. She moans at the impact of my hand on her perfect ass then slowly lowers herself to my lips. Impatient for her, I grip her ass and bring her to my mouth. She nearly collapses at the first swipe of my tongue. I lick and suck at her sweet little clit until she's crying out, then start fucking her with my tongue like I'm going to with my cock.

"Oh my God!" she squeals as her orgasm builds. "Amos... Amos... oh, please!" she chants my name and begs for release. I grip her ass tight and pull her down onto me, sucking her clit hard. Her entire body shakes as she orgasms in a hot rush.

I roll us so that I'm on top and positioned between her legs. Her pussy swollen pink and wetter than I've ever seen. I stroke her clit with the head of my cock, and she twitches and whimpers.

"Sensitive?" I ask with a smirk. All she can do is nod as she tries to catch her breath. "Good. I'm going to fuck you now, wife."

"Yes... fuck me, husband."

I sink into her inch by inch, filling her with every bit of my thick cock. Her pussy pulses around me until I'm using every trick in the book to stave off my own orgasm. I thrust into her hard and fast, rubbing her clit with my fingers until she's screaming my name and clenching around me. There's no holding back. I bury myself deep and come harder than I ever have, then collapse next to her. She rolls into my arms, laying her head over my pounding heart.

"I love you, Amos. I'm sorry I freaked out."

"It's okay, my love. Just talk to me next time. I hope you know I would never do anything to hurt you. You're my heart. My purpose."

We've barely gotten dressed when the sound of a key in the lock comes from the backdoor. Leanne walks in and looks at the kitchen then us. She gives Margo a sly smile then looks at the kitchen again, a little horrified by the mess.

"What happened here?" she finally asks.

"Just a little misunderstanding," Margo responds.

"With the kitchen?" She looks incredulous as she moves toward the counter full of cupcakes. Her focus narrows in what looks like a chocolate cupcake with chocolate icing. "What's this?" she asks Margo.

"Umm... apparently sadness bakes happiness. It's a triple chocolate cupcake filled with strawberry cream and topped with chocolate fudge icing. And it's sinfully good. The best thing I've ever made, I think."

Even though it's five in the morning, Leanne eagerly picks up one of the cakes and takes a huge bite. Her eyes practically roll back in her head at the flavors. Curious, I grab my own cupcake and take a bite. It's delicious. Beyond delicious.

"This is amazing, wife. Like really fucking good," I say around another bite.

Margo's cheeks heat in a blush when Leanne looks at her finger then back at me, quickly putting the pieces together that we are engaged for real this time. "Thanks."

"I want two dozen for the diner," I demand.

She laughs and waves a hand in front of the counter full of cupcakes. "Take your pick. We have dozens of different kinds. I also made a banana parfait cupcake with white chocolate frosting, a burnt sugar cupcake with vanilla cream icing, and pumpkin spice for fall..."

Leanne and I both look at her in awe. "You created four new cupcake flavors in one night?"

She shrugs, "Like I said, sadness bakes happiness."

I shake my head, pulling her close. "Well, you better hope that you get creative happy because that's all you're going to be from now on."

She smiles that bright, beautiful smile I love so much, then turns to Leanne. "You're in charge. I'm going home with my future husband."

Leanne looks at the kitchen then back at us. With a defeated sigh, she waves us away. "Don't worry boss, I'll clean up."

"Thanks."

Fifteen minutes later, we are at home, and I'm throwing my future wife over my shoulder as I carry her up to the house.

"Put me down, you big oaf!" Margo shouts, slapping at my butt as I carry her.

"No way. It's tradition to carry the bride over the threshold."

"Not over your shoulder like a caveman! Plus, we aren't even married."

I slap her ass playfully. "Who says I can't caveman you over the threshold? I think this is perfect. There's no getting away when you're over my shoulder."

She just laughs, wrapping her arms around my waist.

I carry her into the house and straight to our bedroom, then toss her down onto the mattress. She looks up at me with a sexy smile, her eyes dancing with happiness, her cheeks flushed from being over my shoulder. "You're so fucking beautiful."

"I love you, Amos. So much."

I crawl up her body, kissing her deeply. "I'll never stop earning your love."

EPILOGUE

I LOOK IN THE MIRROR, admiring the beautiful white dress I'm wearing. In case you're wondering, it's a wedding dress. Everything has been a whirlwind with Amos and me, including the whole wedding thing. We might've waited, but we both agreed to a quick wedding so that Alan would be able to experience the day while he's still having more good days than bad.

"Oh, honey, you look gorgeous," Trudy says tearfully.

"The dress is perfect," my mom says in agreement with Trudy.

"No tears! I just spent an hour getting her face just right," Lani shouts at the mothers.

I shake my head, my black curls bouncing. That's the one thing Amos requested that my hair be left wild and free. It's definitely wild, though Lani put some kind of cream in it that's tamed the frizziness and made my curls look soft and beautiful.

"Are you sure you want to do this?" Prue asks, giving me the same out she offered Lani before she walked down the aisle to Torin. "I can have the truck pulled around back, and we can bust you out of here."

Ana slaps her arm. "Why are you so anti-marriage?"

Prue snorts, "Haven't you seen how high the divorce rate is? Men are pigs."

"You just wait, Pruette Olsen, one of these days you're going to meet your match, and you'll be eating your words," Lani says.

"It's time, ladies," my dad says.

The wedding is small and brief. We opted to have just close family and friends. And six of those people make up our bridesmaids and groomsmen. Ana grouses as she holds Carson's arm—we may have paired them on purpose, giving them a little push in the right direction... hopefully.

The officiant has us repeat our vows, and then Amos' lips are on mine, and we are pronounced man and wife. The reception is just as small and intimate.

Amos drags me out to dance even though I can't dance at all. Somehow, I manage to not step on his feet as he twirls me around the dancefloor. "Have I told you how beautiful you are?"

I can feel my cheeks heat with a blush. "Once or twice."

"Then definitely not enough. You look phenomenal. All I can think about is flipping that skirt up and licking your hot little pussy until you're screaming my name."

"Yes, please," I say without missing a beat. I'm ready to get this honeymoon started. We discussed having a baby, and I stopped taking my birth control... this is the first week I'm fertile, and I'm ready to start trying for a baby.

Amos throws me over his shoulder and starts carrying me out of the reception hall. "Amos! We can't just leave."

"Sure we can, and we are."

There are woots and claps as he carries me off to our hotel suite. Everyone in the hotel laughs at my husband and me as he strides through the lobby and to the elevators. Inside the elevator, he sets me down long enough to lift me up so I'm hugging him with my thighs. He presses me to the wall and kisses me until there is no breath between us.

When the elevator dings, he carries me with his lips still on mine to our room. He fumbles with the room key for a second, but then he's carrying me over yet another threshold wrong.

"Are you ever going to carry me over the threshold in a normal way?" I ask between kisses.

"No," he growls. "I'm your caveman husband. I want you over my shoulder or over my cock when I carry you off to ravage."

I giggle happily. "Who can argue with that logic."

"I love you, wife of mine."

"I love you too, husband. Now make love to me."

And he does. Over and over until he's certain he planted a baby in me. Only time will tell...

THE END

Find out what happens next for Amos and Margo. Get their bonus story here.

———

Did you miss Lani and Torin's happily ever after? Read it here!

ABOUT THE AUTHOR

Rory Reynolds is a stay-at-home mom of two little monsters. She's a ravenous reader of romance and firmly believes that you can never have too many book boyfriends.

She writes feisty heroines, alpha heroes, and panty drenching smut with happily ever afters.

SUBSCRIBE to my newsletter and get a free book.
http://roryreynoldsromance.com

BB bookbub.com/profile/rory-reynolds
facebook.com/AuthorRoryReynolds
instagram.com/RoryReynoldsBooks

ALSO BY RORY REYNOLDS

Contemporary Romance

Chasing His Forever

Daddy's Temptation

Daddy's Obsession

Daddy's Treat

Daddy's Princess

His Firecracker

His Hellcat

Claiming His Wife

Just Married

Dirty Girl

Dark Contemporary Romance

Unforgettable

Paranormal Romance

Dragon's Thief

Dragon's Curse

Dragon's Hope

Dragon's Ruin

Dragon's Treasure

Dragon's Fire